I0669845

Thomas Cambria Jones

The Last Poems of Thomas Cambria Jones

Thomas Cambria Jones

The Last Poems of Thomas Cambria Jones

ISBN/EAN: 9783741186233

Manufactured in Europe, USA, Canada, Australia, Japa

Cover: Foto ©Andreas Hilbeck / pixelio.de

Manufactured and distributed by brebook publishing software
(www.brebook.com)

Thomas Cambria Jones

The Last Poems of Thomas Cambria Jones

THE

LAST POEMS

OF

THOMAS CAMBRIA JONES,

AUTHOR OF

"MORTALITY: A POEM SUNG IN SOLITUDE."

ETC., ETC., ETC.

Cradled in the Storm.

EDINBURGH:

PRINTED BY BALLANTYNE, ROBERTS, & CO.

1865.

TO MY ILLUSTRIOUS COUNTRYMAN,

JOHN GIBSON, OF ROME.

SCULPTOR who sittest in Art's highest seat,
    Crown'd with the Laurel of undying Fame,
    Let me adorn this page with thy bright Name,
    And place my lowly Book beneath thy feet :
Deal with it as thy judgment deemeth meet.
It humbly greets thee thus :—From Wales I came.
The Mother-Land of men whose earnest aim
Was to advance in glory pure and great—
The Mother-Land of Wilson and of thee.
Read me, O Sculptor, read and ponder o'er
The thoughts my bardic Master sends by me;
And should they tingle through thy quick heart's core,
And claim some nook within thy memory,
Right pleased to hear, indeed, would my old Master be.

CONTENTS.

PROEM.

[Something personal about the Author: how he wrestled with the Evil-power, and how he was called to write "Sermons in Sonnets."]

WHILE I lay in morning slumber,
   Lonely on my quiet bed,
  Various thoughts, a crowding number,
   Took possession of my head :
   Took possession—forced possession—
Vainly strove I 'gainst th' oppression
Of their riot through my head,
While that morning I lay slumb'ring
  Lonely on my quiet bed.

Grief, endured in years early,
  Hemm'd me as of old around ;
And the Power which most unfairly
  Had pursued me like a hound,—
Had pursued—because I would not
Think what my heart's feelings could not
  Without treating Truth as dead,—
Shadow'd me while I lay dreaming
  On my now unquiet bed.

Long I wrestled with the False One,
   That had ever work'd me strife ;
Loud it threaten'd—" One must master—
   Eye for eye, and life for life !"
" *One will master*,—but *thy* servant
I 'd scorn, as *thee* I scorn !" most fervent
   From my heart those words were said ;
Lo, the False One, threat'ning, vanish'd,
   And a light beam'd o'er my bed.

Midst the light a wondrous Creature
   Dawn'd, right palpably to view,
Heavenly—yet of earthly nature,
   With the heavenly shining through :
Shining through the wondrous Creature,
That, as a friend of human nature,
   Smiled on me—but nothing said :
Perhaps the morning Sun was shining
   Brightly o'er my quiet bed. .

While I gazed on this fair vision,—
   If no more than vision 'twere,
I could trace with clear decision
   A Man in the shining air :
Just where erst the wondrous Creature,
That, as a friend of human nature,
   Had smiled on me. The Man then said,
" Why liest thou so long in slumber
   On a dull inglorious bed ?"

I replied, " Oh, I am weary—
   Worn and weary with Art-toil ;
See, there, on my Study's table
   Lies a Palette wet with oil :

Wet with oil, that till 'twas morning,
I bent over—comforts scorning,
  To win independent bread,
Till I sank, oppress'd with languor,
  Lonely on my quiet bed.

" And my scanted rest was broken
  By a rude and ruthless Power ;
Like a hound it hath pursued me
  From my childhood to this hour :
Hath pursued—because I would not
Think what my heart's feelings could not
  Without treating Truth as dead."
Then the Man of God-like nature
  Spake in Song, and thus he said :

" Heed not thou the Power unholy,
  Breaking rudely on thy rest ;
All it loves is sin or folly,
  All that it abhors is blest !

" Heed it not—the Arm is o'er thee,
  Still protecting, as of yore,
When upon the hills which bore thee
  Thou didst wander, lone and poor,

" Thinking not about the morrow,
  But on one melodious Theme,
Weaving o'er thy early sorrow
  All th' enchantment of a dream.

" I was with thee then. Now hear me:
  In the language of the Eld
Let that Theme be woven. Cheer thee !
  Error shall by Truth be quell'd.

" Withering grass and fading flower
    Are but types of earthly things,—
Treasured by the World their hour,
    Then departing, as on wings.

" Lo, THE PRAYER, that shall not perish!
    Take it as thy guiding-star,
And the Good thy Song shall cherish,
    And the Evil shall not mar."

SERMONS IN SONNETS:

ON TEXTS TAKEN FROM THE LORD'S PRAYER.

"Our Father, who art in Heaven."

FOUNTAIN of Life, who wast and will be ever;
From whom proceeds, to whom returns, all
being;
Who lookest down on man — unseen — all
seeing;
Of every fair and goodly thing the Giver—
Of Light, and Air, and Earth, and freshening River;
Agents of Thine, supporting, cheering nature,
Man, and each beast, bird, fish, and creeping creature,
Form'd by Thy will, and therefore form'd not vainly,
But for an End.   O End divine and glorious,
For which all things are made—when Truth victorious,
Shall vanquish Sin and Death—of Mercy telling,
And showing man the ways of wisdom plainly,
Till cleansed from taint, in Truth and Love excelling,
He ripens meet for Thee, Father in Heaven dwelling.

"Hallowed be Thy Name."

FATHER in Heaven, whose Spirit is on earth,
For ever hallow'd be Thy Holy Name !
Kneeling on dust, from which Thou gavest me birth,
Humbly I bow—accept my frail acclaim !
Renew this heart that it unblamed may speak!
Oh, from the Rock Salvation, let gush forth
The healing stream, for I am sore and weak—
Athirst, within life's wilderness, I ache,
And wait the promised aid, which Thou hast said
Shall comfort those who mourn.   Within me, make
The new birth unto Rightcousness complete,
That I may live with Thee—to all else dead—
And walk rejoicing to the radiant Seat,
Prepared for those by whom Thy Name is hallowèd.

"Thy Kingdom come."

DAY hath its dawn, and Earth her infancy.
The clouds,—which have for ages overhung
The world with darkness, whilst the nations rung
With violence, and war, and misery,—
Are breaking—passing from the eastern sky !
For unto us, who mourn'd 'neath night, hath risen
A Light that shall o'erspread the quicken'd land,
And sanctify mankind.   As from a prison,
There shall come forth a freed and cleansèd Band,
A family of God in *thought* and *deed,*
O'er whom pleased Heaven shall smile, and Angels stand
Delighted to behold !   By God's right hand,
The serpent's head is crush'd through Woman's seed :
Oh, hasten, Lord, Thy cause ! Thy Kingdom, Jesus, speed !

" **Thy Will be done on Earth as it is in Heaven.** "

Thy Will is not men's will.   They are perverse
And disobedient children to Thy love ;
They fashion idols of their lusts, and move
And bow to them—deeming Thy rod a curse
When Thou wouldst call their thoughts to Thee, above.
The will of men still strives, as erst it strove,
'Gainst Thee and Thine—to all that 's Good averse :
For it is not Thy Will that gaudy weeds
Should ever crush aside Thy fairest flowers,—
That worthless men, scarr'd with unholy deeds,
Should ever revel in proud halls and towers,
Whilst Worth neglected pines where Want devours,
And the heart utters, as it beats and bleeds,
Would that Thy Will were done in this rude world of ours !

" **Give us this day our daily Bread.** "

Things but abide their season.   Sin and Wrong
Have been permitted to molest the Earth,
From which life's various sufferings have birth ;
But we must war against them with a strong
And never-fainting Faith, that they ere long
Shall be as weeds uprooted and cast forth.
Amidst the battle let this prayer and song
Be alway with our heart, and duly said :
O God ! O Father ! in the needful hour,
For mind and body send our daily bread,
And ever shield us from the Evil-power.
Elijah by the brook was timely fed ;
The Lions' rage was tamed and made to cower :
Behold, the Angel's near !   The Ravens are not dead !

"𝔉orgive us our trespasses, as we forgive them who trespass
against us."

And hast thou pray'd unheeded and unheard ?
And hast thou knock'd at an unopening door ?
The fault is thine—it poisons thy heart's core ;
Thy prayer was not in *spirit*, but in *word:*
And vainly didst thou take the name of Lord ;
And thou didst knock not lowly like the Poor.
Cleanse, cleanse thy heart from all that is impure !
Cleanse it from lust that kindles deeds abhorr'd,—
From pride that doth engender deadliest Sin ;
Forgive thy erring brother —love him more—
To cast a stone how canst *thou* first begin ?
Wrench from the Earth, and place in Heaven, thy store:
Now ask forgiveness in the Name adored ;
Knock ! knock ! it opens : lo, the Saviour hails thee in !

"𝔏ead us not into 𝔗emptation."

Thou art now of the freed and cleansèd Band,
The family of God in *thought* and *deed*,
Whose City 's built upon a Hill, and freed
From this world's bondage ; her foundations stand
Firm on the Rock of Truth—and not on sand ;
Her thoughts are in her holy deeds display'd ;
Yet slumber not—of self, frail self, take heed.
Should chaff appear, the wheat must be refann'd ;
Should dross be found, the gold repass'd through fire ;
'Tis therefore that Temptation hand in hand
With mortal Life doth wend.   Not, not in ire,
But in Thy love and righteous mercy bland,
Lead us to Thee, most holy Lord and Sire,
For we are Thine, and fain would live 'neath Thy command.

"Deliver us from Evil."

WITHOUT lurks Evil. Whatsoever tends
To lure the heart from God is of her brood;
She erst made Paradise a solitude,
And discord belch'd to earth's remotest ends;
And separated hearts of loving friends;
With hatred burning 'gainst the Pure and Good
She reach'd the brand that stream'd a brother's blood.
To her Cain bent—the seed of Cain still bends—
And blood appeals to God. Flee, Child of Wrath,
Flee to the City on the Hill that's freed
From this world's bondage—faint not on thy path;
There is a Shelter free to all who need:
Time or Eternity none other hath—
There tears shall cease to flow, and hearts to ache and bleed.

"Thine is the Kingdom, the Power, and the Glory, for ever."

THINE is the Kingdom, JESUS, glorified,
In which the will of Heaven is done on earth;
And Thou didst visit us of lowly birth!
Wert born of Woman,—wept—taught—bless'd—and died!
When the dark grave by Thee was sanctified,
From Death's cold womb undying Life came forth—
Thou didst uprise 'midst arch-angelic mirth,
And to a banish'd World threw open wide
Thy Father's house, that all might enter there.
WELCOME! throughout the Heaven of heavens resounded;
And through the eternal Universe of prayer— .
Thine is the Kingdom! Glory hails the Heir!
All hail, Pure God the Son—of Power unbounded—
The Whole, the Whole is Thine: on THEE for ever founded.

Amen.

Robert Burns:

25TH OF JANUARY, A.D. 1859.

GAZE back a century ago,
   As yesterday it seems in Time,
To where you mountains clad with snow,
   Watch o'er stern Scotia's stormy clime,
Recalling deeds which brightly throw
Their lustre on the vales below.

Beneath you mountains bleak and wild,
   Which murmur many a wintry tune,
A straw-thatch'd cottage stands up-piled,
   Close to the banks of river Doon,
And there a peasant clasps his child—
A first-born son—his undefiled.

What blessings hath the mother won,
   While from her couch of straw she sees
The tender father clasp her son
   In fond parental ecstasies ;
And, though a peasant, deem the boon
The best that Heaven could send him down.

And so it was.   A hundred years
   Has measured out its days since then,
And lo ! that peasant's son appears
   A Chief among the chief of men ;
Whose name each way-worn brother cheers,
And man to man exalts—endears.

Breathe but the name of Robert Burns,
　　High feelings vibrate at the sound,—
The wanderer to his country turns,
　　And home and kindred gather round,—
For *Auld Lang Syne* his bosom yearns,
And gross or selfish joy he spurns.

Breathe but his name—the Songs uprise,
　　Familiar now through every land ;
From Land of Cakes to where the skies
　　Pour down their glare o'er burning sand,
The human heart responsive sighs,
Or gladdens with his melodies.

The lady sings them in her bower,
　　The baron in his castle proud,
The beggar in his jollier hour,
　　The ballad-monger in the crowd,—
The Poet glories in their power,
And tyrants feel their truth, and— cower.

Pale students on them musing pore ;
　　Fresh offerings grace the Poet's brow ;
Gray sages marvel at the lore
　　Of one who whistled at the plough,
And from their schools the laurel tore,
And wreath'd it his own temples o'er.

'Twas nobly taken, justly won :
　　Bright be that Laurel evermore !
All honour to the peasant's Son,
　　Whose Fame has dawn'd o'er sea and shore,
Whose free and truthful thoughts are sown
Wherever Heaven's blest light shines on.

Whose Fame has *dawn'd* o'er shore and sea,
  Prophetic of a day at hand,
When, from those truthful thoughts which he
  Broadcast o'er an unheeding land,
Harvest is ripe—how great will be
The day that gen'rous Fame will see !

Th' *Illustrious* of his native soil
  Were blind, or idly closed their eyes ;
Choice fare was theirs—bread, wine, and oil—
  All, all that selfish natures prize—
Whilst he, the glory of their Isle,
Was famishing.   Does Scotland smile ?

Alas ! 'twas ever thus, and we
  Must pity and forgive—forget
We dare not—cannot : every tree
  Yields its own fruit ; nor can we yet
Find grapes on thistles.   Let it be
A lesson to futurity.

The worldly love the world.   His love
  Is sun-like—blesses all around—
Brings down a glory from above,
  And makes earth consecrated ground ;
It shines where'er his fancies rove—
Therein his feelings breathe and move.

He came not for one class of men,
  Nor for one land, nor for one age—
His mission was to all.   Within
  Glow'd Heaven, and sanctified the rage
Wherewith he strove to rend the chain
That link'd his brother man to Pain.

Song found him musing at the plough ;
  The humble hinds first hail'd his voice :
Next Learning sought him ; then, as now.
  He made the best of hearts rejoice ;
And titled crowds, having seen the show,
To Genius made their farewell bow.[1]

Dumfries contains the Poet's dust ;
  Men hold the treasures of his mind ;
He needs no monumental bust
  To rank him from the common kind ;
Heaven shields his soul among her Just :
Men will preserve their sacred trust.

From Land of Cakes to Snowdon's brow,
  From Snowdon's brow to Famma's cone,
From Famma's cone to Lapland's snow,
  From Lapland to the burning Zone,
Honour to Robert Burns will flow :
MIND IS THE IMAGE OF GOD BELOW.

———◆———

To Queen Victoria.[2]

ON THE ROYAL VISIT TO THE PRINCIPALITY.

HAIL ! mighty Sovereign of the brave,
  Whose flag on every sea
Proclaims sweet freedom to the slave,
  Whate'er his colour be ;
And to the oppress'd—no matter whom
Holds out protection and a home.

Thou art a Vict'ry over War,
  Blest sunshine after storm ;
In thy calm time the heavenly Star
  Of Peace displays her form,
And showers below the golden seeds
Of glorious thoughts and righteous deeds.

High Art, Philosophy, and Song,
  Which sanctify the sod,
Are honour'd now thy Isles among
  As Blessings sent from God :
For thou dost love them—and to thee
MIND IS THE TRUE NOBILITY.

And this, true Lady, spreads thy name
  From clime to clime afar,
And lightens through all hearts a flame
  Time cannot dim or mar ;
To others slaves may bend their knee,
But the heart bounds to bow to thee.

We therefore hail thee, gracious Queen,
  To this ne'er-conquer'd Strand,
Where Health and Beauty, most serene,
  And Toil, dance hand in hand ;
Where erst the noblest men had birth
Who e'er adorn'd the peopled earth.

Gaze on our Vales—by virtue charm'd—
  Renown'd in Song and Art ;
Where glides the Clwyd 'tween banks well farm'd,
  Skill'd Agriculture's mart ;
There Inigo to science sprung—[3]
There lovely Hemans lived and sung.[4]

Gaze on our Hills, from Famma's cone,
  'Neath which lies Wilson's grave,[5]
To Snowdon's brow, and say, fair One,
  'Mongst all the bright and brave
Where flourishes the favour'd strand
That supersedes this ancient land.

Think o'er our Past—nay, startle not,
  Mild Lady, 'tis the shout
Of loyal hearts which crowd each spot,
  And what they feel springs out :
Think on our Sires—what once they were
Their Children are who hail thee here.

———◆——

Ode for the 10th March, A.D. 1863.

TO THE PRINCE OF WALES.

Prince of the loyal Isle,
Where Valour, nursed 'neath Freedom's smile,
  Invincible and bold,
Shielded from hostile band
The homes of our dear mountain Land
  In rudest times of old ;
Where Bards breathed forth the deathless voice
  Of patriotic Song,
And made the public heart rejoice
  In all that did belong
To Wales the Blest, whose noblest choice
  We rank thee now among !

To the Prince of Wales.

Our royal Harp is heard,
  Fresh founts of hope and joy have stirr'd
    On this thy bridal-day !
We hail the peerless Bride
Thou hast brought home to be our pride—
    To elevate and sway ;
She leaves the charms of northern skies,
  And braves a heaving sea—
An Angel, in fair woman's guise,
  She comes with love to thee ;
And, in the heaven of her eyes,
  Our future Queen we see.

War's savage reign is o'er ;
Peace pours around her golden store,
    And wreathes the throne with Flowers !
Upward to thee we gaze :
Love Wales in act that love displays,—
    Arouse her slumb'ring powers !
To Song, Philosophy, and Art,
  From which true glory springs,
Thy princely smile and aid impart !
  Wales to the *noble* clings—
Thou wilt be shrined within her heart,
  Descendant of our Kings.

Bridal Song.

AWAKE, Harp of Wales, from the night of thy slumbers,
   And pour through our valleys the warm soul of Song,
'Till Snowdon resound with the spell of thy numbers,
   And Echo repeats it her hoar rocks among.
A good time awaits thee, ancient Harp of the free-born,
   Thy night shall disperse like the mist from the hill,
As thy woods become vocal, and Morn is in glee born,
   While Nature rejoices and throws off her chill.

A blue April sky expands o'er the Mansion
   Of Kinmel the princely, the pride of the land;
And that glorious Arch of ethereal expansion
   By the bow of our Hope in the future is spann'd.
The sky has no gloom, and the blithe Sun shines brightly
   O'er garlands which blossom in perfume around,
And the frolicking breeze, as in breathing by lightly,
   Brings merrily onward the bridal-peal's sound.

And warm loving hearts in the village are meeting,
   Thy name, Abergele,[6] they'll treasure henceforth;
Oh, long will they think of the bliss in thus greeting
   The union of Beauty, Love, Virtue, and Worth.
And here's to the Bride—may her morning of beauty
   Glide cloudless in joy to the heavenly strand!
And here's to the Bridegroom—our affection and duty—
   And Kinmel the princely, the pride of the land.

—<★≍◉≍≍◉≍★—

𝔎𝔦𝔫𝔪𝔢𝔩 𝔅𝔦𝔯𝔱𝔥𝔡𝔞𝔶 𝔖𝔬𝔫𝔤.

A Song for the day that to Kinmel has given
    An Heir to her house and her kingly domains ;
O Child of the Mother-Land, favour'd of Heaven,
    A prayer for thee rises from mountains and plains ;
Sweet be thy slumbers—may the nurse-songs sung o'er thee
    Ever nurture thy love to the Land of thy birth,
And picture the Good and Heroic before thee,
    Who beam'd, as from heaven, a sunshine on earth.

Blest be thy young dreams—and when manhood awakes thee
    To the calls of thy rank, and high duties of life,
In the morn of thy days, ere Night overtakes thee,
    May Truth be thy brave banner through warfare and strife.
And deep in thy heart be this wise motto treasured,
    The words which our famed Druid-Bards sung of yore,
Heb Dduw, Heb Ddim : Duw a Digon ![7] the unmeasured
    Abundance of heaven shall then be thy store.

The Sun shines on Kinmel, bright garlands surround her,
    As she stands in her beauty of place by the sea ;
The hearts of the people out-speak what they've found her—
    All noble in feeling—good, gracious, and free.
Hurrah for the day that to Kinmel has given
    An Heir to her house and her kingly domains !
And Health to the Child, with the blessing of Heaven !
    Is the prayer that now rises from mountains and plains.

𝔄 𝔅𝔞𝔟𝔢 𝔖𝔪𝔦𝔩𝔦𝔫𝔤 𝔦𝔫 𝔖𝔩𝔢𝔢𝔭.

"Of such is the Kingdom of God."—St Luke.

That smile of thine is not of earth,
Of this world's evil or its worth,
Or of its sorrow or its mirth,—
   Thou hast no thought.
Fair Babe, from heaven so newly come,
Its glory, purity, and bloom
Cling to thee in the lowly home
   Which thou hast sought.

Thanks ever for the lore divine,
Reveal'd by that bland smile of thine !
Thou seest !—alas, these eyes of mine
   But blindly see.
Thou hearest !—but *in part* I hear,
A grosser world disturbs my ear—
The hymn of Truth's melodious sphere
   Is heard by thee.

The Kingdom's bright and clear before thee :
And a voice says—*I will restore thee !*
Thou seest fair Angels watching o'er thee,
   And know'st no fear.
Oh, ever may that smile of thine,
Enshrined within this heart of mine,
Remind me of the lore divine,—
   That Heaven is near.

SONNETS.

𝔉uneral 𝔖onnet:

SIR JOHN HAY WILLIAMS, BART., A.D. 1859.

WE do not mourn like those whose Hope has perish'd ;
　The sinking Sun that sets will rise again :
　Though clouds obscure its light, it knows no stain ;
And the blest Faith that in our heart is cherish'd
　Extends beyond the mists of Death's domain.
　Refined and purified by fleshly pain,
　The Christian ripens meet to join the Just;
　His Faith is strength in weakness,—Life in Death !
　And the great Song of triumph,—Dust to Dust—
An Angel is released from bonds and breath !
　Seek ye the Record of his days ? 'tis here,
A LIFE WELL SPENT IN DEEDS OF LOVE AND WORTH ;
　The grateful Poor proclaim it with a tear :
Can all thy wealth bestow a purer tribute, Earth ?

𝔉uneral 𝔖onnet:

THE PRINCE CONSORT, A.D. 1861.

THROUGHOUT the land men's inner thoughts are stirr'd,
　As though a star had fallen from on high,
　Leaving in heaven a dreary vacancy ;
Forth from the nation's heaving heart is heard
　A sigh of earnest mourning, and the cry—
　DEATH ! DEATH ! is echoed to the furthest sky.
Death pass'd the cottage door without a word,
　Knock'd at the palace gate, and said : " I wait,
　Albert, I wait : the Night hath come—the gate

Of life is closing : Joys which flesh holds dear
   Thine eyes I seal from : all that's goodly great
Will ever live where I shall *not* appear."
   God shield our widow'd Queen ! hearts heave and beat:
We Sin, and Death is nigh ; we Pray, and God is near.

Mary's Fount,

SAINT ASAPH.

It was a goodly thought thus to up-bring,
   Into our little City on the hill,
   The treasure of fair Elwy's generous rill.
Henceforth of thanks a grateful offering
Will duly flow, as freely as the Fount
   Pours its pure stream the well-pleased City through,
To him, who, mindful of a public want,
   Gave a substantial form that thought unto.
A future age to Mary's Fount will come
   And drink its water, (when we thirst no more,)
Blessing the Memory of her whose Tomb,
That lies near Isaac Barrow's burial-bed,
   Is daily deck'd with flowers from Love's rich store,
Revealing more than words may utter of the Dead.

A Birthday Festival.

Scene,   .   The Bishop's Palace, Saint Asaph.
Time,   .   The 16th of September, A.D. 1860.

A Blessed Sun smiles on the loving earth :
   Threescore and ten of ancient People meet,

With joyous hearts, to celebrate and greet
The day that gave their Host and Guardian birth
Just seventy years ago.   Oh, act of worth,
   To call together thus the agèd poor
As children of one Father—thus to brighten,
   As with a wreath of flowers, their cottage door,
Those loving lowly hearts which beat and lighten,
   In grateful gladness blithely flowing o'er,
   And in true prayer, which dies not with the breath,
But will bring down a Blessing that henceforth
   Shall charm the path of him, through life and death,
Who fed those helpless Lambs, and shared their child-
   like mirth.

Birthday Sonnet:

TO THE BISHOP OF SAINT ASAPH.

A WHILE I mused near Isaac Barrow's grave ;
   Reading the pious epitaph thereon,
   How many years, thought I, have come and gone,
Since those respected stones were rear'd, which save
The dust of him whose Christian virtues have
   Beam'd o'er our Church a light that, like the Sun,
   Gladdens all hearts.   Servant of Christ, well done !
Not to the proud but to the Poor he gave :
He lent unto the Lord and is repaid.
   Vain monuments, once here, have sculk'd away,
But Barrow's modest grave is sacred made
   By wisely gracious deeds.   May many a day
Smile over thee as now ere thou art laid,
   In a like-honour'd grave, near thy 'loved Barrow's clay.

To Samuel Sebastian Wesley,

THE MUSICIAN.

IF, Wesley, with the Masters of pure Song,
  Thy name is to exist in after-years,
  Thou wilt not grieve beneath the simple sneers,
Which now assail thee from a scribbling throng
Of men, who cannot owe thee grudge or wrong ;
  Unless beyond their cramp'd and petty spheres
Thou hast aspired to soar, and nobly sought
That sacred Mount to which the great belong :
  Handel, Beethoven, Spohr, thy 'loved compeers
Hymn'd freely there the melodies of thought
  Which now enchant Mankind. Heed not vain jeers,
  Nor meet infuriated rage with ire ;
Be true to thy high Art—proceed—dread nought :
  'Tis dross, not gold, that perishes in fire.

Opening of Ruthin Railway,

ST DAVID'S DAY, A.D. 1860.

To James Maurice, Esq.

JOY to thy heart, my friend, and to thy town,
  Ruthin, whom thou hast toil'd for long and well ;
  Of whose heroic *yore* War's records tell ;
Whose prosperous *future* this crown'd day makes known.
She now will reap the harvest wisely sown
  By thee and thy compeers. The happy Vale
Shouts forth with joy—proud Famma's stately cone
Resounds ten thousand voices blent in one.

And Clwyd, rejoicing through each mead and dale,
　Where Beauty seats herself as on a throne,
　Seems thus with Song to charm the passing gale :
The work of War is over, the hireling's paid and gone,—
Hang out the banner of holy Peace with these words in-
　　scribed thereon :
ART, SCIENCE, TRUE LABOUR, FREE COMMERCE, AND EVERY
　　MAN HIS OWN.

The Good Old Town:

9TH OF NOVEMBER, A.D. 1862.[9]

JOY to the good old Town !
　The Bells peal out aloud,
From their Tower of renown,
　O'er a rejoicing crowd ;
And zealous hearts exclaim,
　As that merry peal rings down,—
" Hurrah for the coming time !
　Joy to the good old Town !"

O Wrexham, far renown'd !
　Fair Queen of all the North !
Of yore thy brow was crown'd
　For Beauty, Truth, and Worth ;
Well have thy Sons this day,
　Their Sires' stanch spirit shown ;
Hark ! far-off voices say,
　" Well done the good old Town !"

Twas not for *red* or *white*
   The battle has been won,
But to protect the Right
   Of Cottage, Hall, and Throne.
Honour to whom 'tis due ;
   Let each man have his own :
Wrexham, thou hast been true—
   Joy to the good old Town !

God speed thy coming time !
   Greatly uphold thy brow,
And beautify our clime
   With thoughts and deeds which glow.
Learning and Science fair
   Be thine ; cast Evil down ;
This is the Poet's prayer—
   Joy to the dear old Town !

Shakespeare :

THE 23D OF APRIL, A.D, 1864.

Prologue: spoken in Wrexham Theatre.

THERE needs no trumpet to proclaim the name
Of him whom Milton hails, *Great Heir of Fame;*
The Bard, who on the banks of Avon breathed
   His first and last of human life, and there
Buried, for favour'd Stratford has enwreath'd
   Endearment and renown, a garland rare ;
And to mankind of every grade and clan,
Bequeathed a treasure that ennobles man :
Strength to the weak, true guidance to the strong,—
The wisdom of all time embalm'd in Song.

Ye sons and daughters of the dear old Town,
Wrexham, the Pride of Wales, for worth well known,
Assembled here, on this day set apart
In Memory of him whose Throne 's the heart,
Shakespeare, for evermore a deathless voice—
Shakespeare, in whom the Nations now rejoice,—
Your kind indulgence let me humbly ask
For those who undertake the arduous task
To picture forth the scenes his Genius drew,
And bring his bright creations to your view.

This favour ask'd 'tis needless more to say,
So bowing grateful thanks I go my way,
For Wrexham hearts are generous to the core,
And when the best is done, expect no more.

In Remembrance:

JOHN ROBERTS, ESQ., OF RHUDDLAN ABBEY, A.D. 1862.

Who claim the tears of Song, the embalming tears of Song,
When man is laid in the Churchyard-bed, where night and
 sleep are long,
Until the bright Morn of Judgment breaks o'er Christ's
 victorious Throng?

Not they whose selfish days were spent in feast and revelry;
Not they who hoarded up rich store whilst the starved were
 fainting by;
Not they whose titles were the sole pledge of their nobility.

For thee—rare man of humble birth, untitled, and unknown,
Save by the Crown thy gracious deeds unvauntingly have
 won—
Widow and Orphan record the tale of Christian duties done.

For thee the tears of Song will flow, the embalming tears of
    Song,
And refresh the flowers strewn on thy grave, where night
    and sleep are long,
Until the bright Morn of Judgment breaks o'er Christ's
    victorious Throng.

A Song for the Toiling Man.

A Song for the toiling Man,
Who labours while he can,
For a little needful bread,
And a shelter for his head :
    Be patient—persevere.

Grieve not the Wine 's denied ;
There 's a well on every side,
Whose water 's ever free,
Even Man of Toil for thee :
    And thou hast naught to fear.

There quench thy thirst in peace ;
Let fleshly passion cease
To torture Truth astray—
In Truth and Spirit pray :
    Earnestly pray and crave.

Pray for the Truth that flows
From heaven to earth, and goes
From earth to heaven again
With unprison'd souls from pain :
    Ask—and thou shalt receive.

C

There is a wondrous Spring
For Sinners perishing
With spiritual thirst, and those
Who drink thereof repose,
  And never thirst again.

And Christ, thy God, and Friend,
Will on thee there attend :
Oh, haste and drink, and Life,
Victor o'er Death and Strife,
  And cleansed from sinly stain,

Will evermore be thine.
Be this Life thine and mine ;
Then though we toil for bread,
And a shelter for the head,
  We live not here in vain.

An Epitaph

THAT HAS NOT APPEARED ON A TOMBSTONE.

HE eat—he drank—he slept.   What then ?
He awoke, eat, drank, and slept again :
Such was his life for threescore years and ten.

Vanity and Reality.

" Vanity of vanities, saith the Preacher, vanity of vanities ; all is
vanity."—ECCLESIASTES.

VANITY of vanities ! so spake the Preacher-King,
Surrounded by the pomp of wealth and every precious thing ;
Whate'er the heart desired was his, and his this solemn cry :
Vanity of vanities—all, all is vanity !

In kingly guise he sat amidst the splendour of his throne,
The beauty of the Beautiful he fed his eyes upon ;
He call'd around him all the Wise, the Cunning, and the
    Strong :
Yet vanity of vanities, was the burthen of his Song.

He gazed beyond the ken of kings—Earth's Beautiful and
    Fair
He found were frail and perishing—all fleshly joys were care ;
The Wise, the Cunning, and the Strong, but made his heart
    to ache :
Their lore, their handicraft, and feats, seem'd hollow, vain,
    and weak.

He felt a *power* beyond afar the strength of earthly arm ;
He saw a *craft* compared with which all others ceased to
    charm ;
He heard a *voice*, a higher voice than this world's boasted
    lore :
Reality, Reality surrounds him evermore.

𝔍𝔬𝔥𝔫 𝔐𝔞𝔯𝔱𝔦𝔫'𝔰 𝔊𝔯𝔞𝔳𝔢.[10]

ADDRESSED TO A FRIEND AT SAINT ASAPH.

FROM Mona's Isle, where lately I have wander'd,
    Accept this verse, my heart's harmonious friend,
Not as a theme that has been overponder'd,
    But on the roadside rudely thought and penn'd.

Little I deem'd when last we sat together
    Within thy tasteful room, and spoke of Art
And her great Masters, whilst the wintry weather
    Bellow'd out-doors with many a fitful start;

And Martin's grand creations hanging 'round us,
    Threw their poetic light throughout the room,
Till, as a wizard's spell, his Genius bound us,—
    That I should write to thee on Martin's tomb!

A few weeks ere I sought this peaceful Island,
    He died near Douglas, to which place he came
In hopes a lingering sickness to beguile, and
    Braddan now holds his dust and shares his fame.

'Tis a most pleasant spot where he lies sleeping,
    Upon a gentle hill, around it heave
The Mountains which he loved, most meetly keeping
    A solemn Wake above his lowly grave:

And at his head two little trees are springing,
    And on those trees two little Birds I see,
And those sweet Birds unitedly are singing,
    And thus I give their Song, my friend, to thee:

"O highly-favour'd Braddan, keep thy treasure !
　The dust of Princes is but common dust,—
Fame unto them is measured as they measure :
　The Sculptor claims the praise, the Prince the bust !

"The honour'd dust that here with thee's reposed
　Was of a loftier order,—it contain'd
A Soul that glanced through nature, and disclosed
　To marvelling men the simple and the train'd,

"Scenes of surpassing grandeur, which for ever
　Will haunt their memories ; and there will come,
From far-off lands, the Gifted and the Clever,
　To gaze in silent thought upon this tomb."

The Last Visions of John Martin.

[Through the kindness of a friend, an opportunity was afforded me for leisurely inspecting the three final efforts of Martin's genius—"*The Last Judgment*," "*The Great Day of His Wrath*," and "*The Plains of Heaven*." The sentiment with which those Paintings impressed my mind gave birth to the present Poem.]

Invocation.

BROTHER in spirit, though happily not in fate,
Of exiled Dante, who with solemn lays
Lifted his voice against the guilty days
'Midst which he lived ; lest I of aught misstate,
Whilst from thy hieroglyphics I translate
The vast Design that fills me with amaze,
Stream'd from thy mind with skill most consummate,

I crave the aid of those pure Plains of Light,
Which unto thee are no more dimly seen,
Where now thou dwell'st 'neath thy Redeemer's sight.
True Fame has crown'd thee with her evergreen,
And placed thy name among the Wise and Bright :
Prophet, and Bard, and Sage, who fought the fight of Right.

FIRST PICTURE.

The Last Judgment.

THE Trumpet has been heard : from far and near
Both Quick and Dead assemble at the call ; [11]
Before Christ's throne th' adoring Elders fall ; [12]
Two Books within two Angels' hands appear :
The Book of Life is opened wide, and there
The names endure that Hell cannot appal ;
The Book of Death is closed, and therein all
Whose god was Antichrist recorded are—
Gross worshippers of Earth and fleshly power,
Who against Truth have warr'd, and blindly stroven
To kill man's inner Life. The final hour
Of Time has toll'd.   In twain the World is cloven :
Cleansed from Sin's taint the Good receive their dower,
And th' Evil wailing rage while Conscience does devour.

SECOND PICTURE.

The Great Day of His Wrath.

Lo, the Sun darkens o'er Jerusalem, [13]
Henceforth another light is hers.   The Moon [14]
'Midst blood wanes in the trembling horizon :
She saw the vain attempts (and weeps for them)
Made by Earth-worshippers the diadem
Of ancient Faith in sport to trample on.

Where has the pride of Gog and Magog gone ? [15]
An Earthquake's arm did its frail fury stem,
On the four winds the Trumpet loud resounded ;
And cleansing Wrath from Heaven has swept forth
In lightnings fierce and thunders, which rebounded
Where'er the Accursed sought refuge. Mother Earth,
Protect thy worshippers ! The Earth, astounded,
Convulsive gasps, and dies with all upon her founded.

" In Mount Zion and in Jerusalem there shall be deliverance."—
Joel ii. 32.

And Zion rises crown'd with holy light
Beam'd from the City glorified above ;
There Christ's assembled People reign in love :
Of every age the Just, the Wise, and Bright :
There, in the Hymn commenced on Earth, unite
Angelo—Milton—Socrates, who strove
Against corruption ; Dante, who could move,
By living verse, the persecuting spite
Of men who play'd Religion as a game ;
There Raffaelle, Dürer, Wilson, and Lorraine,
Who lit Art's altar with ethereal flame ;
Handel, Mozart, Beethoven, whose rapt strain
Tingled through savage hearts and made them tame ;
And thousands more were there, known and unknown to
    Fame.

THIRD PICTURE.

The Plains of Heaven.

Thanks to thee, Painter-Poet, for the treasure
That thou revealest here to mortal eyes,
Which John, enrapt with holy ecstasies,
At Patmos saw—beyond all human measure—

The new Jerusalem adorn'd with leisure,
Even as a Bride to meet her husband sighs,
Descending from on high amidst the cries
Of that great voice he heard announce with pleasure :
The Tabernacle of God shall be henceforth
With men—its final, sure, and blest abode ;
And He shall dwell with them on a new Earth ;
And they shall be His people ; He their God !
Sorrow and Death are lost in heavenly mirth :
The former things are changed—this is the latter Birth.

Thanks to thee, Painter-Poet,—evermore
Of this high lesson thou remindest me,
Life over Death triumphant is to be !
And hark, the Harp resounds—— 'long yonder shore
The Song of Heaven is heard.   Faith's fight is o'er !
Behold, HE reigns, whom, erst on Calvary,
Men smote and pierced, and crown'd in mockery !
Now Jew and Gentile, of all times, adore
The CHRIST that rescued man from Death and Hell.
O Christian Reader, o'er these solemn lays
Inwardly ponder—self and passion quell ;
And till we meet before the Throne of Praise,
Where holy Love and Song for ever dwell,
Till then, whoe'er thou art, Peace to thee, and Farewell.

NOTES.

Robert Burns.

NOTE 1, PAGE 19.

And titled crowds, having seen the show,
To Genius made their farewell bow.

I have met two persons who had been personally acquainted with Robert Burns, and lived at Dumfries during the Poet's time. One was Mr Allan Cunningham, to whom, in 1823, I was introduced at Sir Francis Chantrey's, the Sculptor; the other, an old gentleman named Clark, for whose acquaintance, in 1834, I was indebted to Mr Egerton Smith of Liverpool. Both Cunningham and Clark united in stating that Burns was coldly received by fair-weather friends on his second visit to Edinburgh, and utterly deserted by them towards the close of his life.

Ode to Queen Victoria.

NOTE 2, PAGE 19.

Should this Ode to our gracious Queen, and the following one to His Royal Highness Albert Edward, Prince of Wales, be honoured some auspicious morning by the perusal of those exalted personages to whom they are right loyally addressed, they may probably be a humble means of awaking influential consideration to the expediency of fitting-up Carnarvon Castle, wherein our first Prince of English parents was born, as a royal residence for our present Prince, and for all future Heirs-apparent of England's throne.

NOTE 3, PAGE 20.

There Inigo to science sprung.

In my boyhood I have heard it frequently stated, by aged people of Wrexham and neighbourhood, that Inigo Jones, the famous architect, and wit-rival of rare Ben Jonson, was born at old Brymbo Hall, and that the Hall now standing was built from his design. But it is more generally believed in the Principality that Inigo was a native of the vale of Clwyd. The Register reported to have been lately discovered is only evidence that he was christened—not born—in London. Mention has been made of an Altar-piece, painted by him when a youth, preserved in a Church not far from the Vale.

He lived much of his time in London, where he died and was buried.

NOTE 4, PAGE 20.

There lovely Hemans lived and sung.

Felicia Hemans, the poetess, of whom Byron, William Wordsworth, and Walter Scott make honourable mention, lived the brightest years of her life near Saint Asaph, on the banks of the River Clwyd. The Cathedral Church here holds a few modest inches of marble erected to her memory. She died in Dublin, and was buried there, A.D. 1835.

NOTE 5, PAGE 21.

Gaze on our Hills, from Famma's cone,
'Neath which lies Wilson's grave.

Richard Wilson, the most illustrious landscape-painter of ancient or modern times, on whose Genius public opinion, at home and abroad, has been long since unequivocally pronounced, was born at Penegoes, Machynlleth, of which place his father was Rector. The present Penegoes Rector informs me that the father's signature as *John Willson, Rector,* occurs in the Church-Register there from 1722 to 1729. Wilson died at Colomendy Hall, and lies buried in Mold, a town at the foot of Moel Famma. When I visited the Hall in 1825, the treasured bed of this Apostle of Art was shown to me—the bed on which Wilson breathed his last of human life.

Bridal Song.

NOTE 6, PAGE 23.

And warm loving hearts in the village are meeting,
The name Abergele they'll treasure henceforth.

This Song was sung at the marriage-festivals of Hugh Robert Hughes, Esq., of Kinmel Park, held in Abergele and other places, on the 18th of April, A.D. 1853.

Kinmel Birthday Song.

NOTE 7, PAGE 24.

The words which our famed Druid-Bards sung of yore,
Heb Dduw, Heb Ddim : Duw a Digon!

This ancient Welsh, which I find retained on the Kinmel seal, may be thus rendered—SANS GOD, SANS GOOD : GOD AND PLENTY.

Birthday Sonnet.

NOTE 8, PAGE 23.

May many a day
Smile over thee as now, ere thou art laid
In a like-honour'd grave, near thy 'loved Barrow's clay.

The well-preserved tombstone of this goodly Churchman is on the right-hand side of the state entrance into Saint Asaph Cathedral Church.   Facing ·Barrow's tombstone, on the left, there is one of similar construction to the memory of Mrs Mary Short.   Barrow was translated from the Isle of Man to St Asaph in 1669, and died, as his pious and quaintly beautiful epitaph expresses—*On the Feast of St John the Baptist, in the year of our Lord* 1680 ; *aged* 67.

He remembered the forgotten, and was a friend to the friendless. By his Christian beneficence St Asaph Almshouses were erected.

The Good Old Town:

9TH OF NOVEMBER, A.D. 1862.

NOTE 9, PAGE 30.

On this day John Lewis, Esq., of Rhos-ddu Lodge, was elected Mayor of Wrexham, and re-elected the following year.

John Martin's Grave.

NOTE 10, PAGE 30.

"BALLACARNEY HOUSE, ST JOHN'S, ISLE OF MAN,
May 1854.

"The other day I visited the grave of our remarkable painter, John Martin. He departed this life at six o'clock P.M., the 17th day of February last, aged 65, at the house, so I am informed, of a marriage-relative named Wilson, situated on a cliff overlooking the town of Douglas. Enclosed you will receive a copy of some verses which were composed at the time of my visit. Perhaps I should state that the *two little trees* mentioned therein were then, and I trust will continue to be, at the head of the grave. It is customary here to hold a *wake* over the Dead. The mountains, which are supposed in my verse to hold their solemn wake over the departed Painter, are Snaefell, (the Snowdon of the Isle,) and North and South Barrule."—AUTHOR'S MS. LETTER.

The Last Visions of John Martin.

NOTE 11, PAGE 38.

The Trumpet has been heard : from far and near
Both Quick and Dead assemble at the call.

"And he shall send his angels with a great sound of a trumpet, and they shall gather together his elect from the four winds, from one end of heaven to the other."—MATT. xxiv. 31.

NOTE 12, PAGE 38.

Before Christ's throne th' adoring Elders fall.

"The four and twenty elders fall down before him that sat on the throne, and worship him that liveth for ever and ever."—REV. iv. 10.

NOTE 13, PAGE 38.

Lo, the Sun darkens o'er Jerusalem,
Henceforth another Light is hers.

"And there shall be no night there; and they need no candle, neither light of the sun; for the Lord God giveth them light : and they shall reign for ever and ever."—REV. xxii. 5.

NOTE 14, PAGE 38.

The Moon
'Midst blood wanes in the trembling horizon.

"The sun shall be turned into darkness, and the moon into blood, before the great and the terrible day of the Lord come."—JOEL ii. 31.

NOTE 15, PAGE 39.

Where has the pride of Gog and Magog gone?
An Earthquake's arm did its frail fury stem.

Martin, in his picture *The Last Judgment*, under the type of Gog and Magog, represents the multitudinous Host of Antichrist,—the congregated infidels of all nations, — passing over the Valley of Jehoshaphat to lay siege to the Holy City. The war-elephants of far-off countries, and railway-trains from the chief cities of civilised society, laden with Warriors whose heart-shout is,—*We will have no Christ to reign over us!* press forward, and lo! the doomed valley is instantly convulsed by earthquake—the proud viaduct that led to Jerusalem is rent in twain—and the pride of Gog and Magog is hurled down, and for ever buried in utter darkness.

THE END.

BALLANTYNE, ROBERTS, AND COMPANY, PRINTERS, EDINBURGH